SHAME MUD

SHAME MUD

Written by Jamie Jensen · Illustrated by Dustin Baird

TRUE WORTH BOOKS

TRUE WORTH BOOKS
True Worth Books LLC
Lehi, Utah USA

ISBN 9780578803418

Printed by Ingram Spark
First printing edition 2021.

Written by Jamie Jensen
Illustration by Dustin Baird

www.trueworthbooks.org

For Declan
— J.J.

For Ivy
— D.B.

Bill rumble-tumbled out his door
To start this special day.
His baseball game was after school.
He could not *wait* to play.

A quick munch crunch; a tender hug–
Mom loved him most, by far.
She breathed in deep. "My Billy boy,
Remember who you are."

At school, he felt excitement spread.
He jumped and sang and skipped.
He didn't notice Jack there and,
He didn't mean to trip.

But trip he did, and hurt he did
When he knocked into Jack.
Jack stomped and yelled, he kicked and wailed,
And gave Bill's arm a smack.

His cheeks were warm, his chest felt tight,
His feet were dragging slow.
He could not bring his head up high.
His heart felt awfully low.

In class he felt a bit more calm
Because there was a quiz.
He did not mind this much at all.
At math – he was a whiz!

But when the test was handed back
There was a big red "C".
His head hung down and Billy thought,
"There's something wrong with me."

His cheeks were warm, his chest felt tight,
His feet were dragging slow.
He could not bring his head up high.
His heart felt awfully low.

At lunch, he thought he could escape
This yucky, gloomy weight.
He looked around for his close friend.
It looked like Finn was late.

When Finn was nowhere to be seen,
Bill felt that he could cry.
Then suddenly, he heard Tom say,
"You should have seen Finn's eye!"

Tom said that he and Finn had been
Out climbing trees to play.
"Finn won't be at the game today.
His eye's a purplish-gray."

Bill stood in shock! He felt surprised,
So lonely, and so down.
And why was he the last to hear?
He could not help but frown.

His cheeks were warm, his chest felt tight,
His feet were dragging slow.
He could not bring his head up high.
His heart felt awfully low.

Outside, the game went pretty well,
Though they were missing Finn.
They played their best and Billy thought,
"I really hope we win."

He had a chance to help his team.
He ran with all his might.
He tried to catch a high fly ball.
It smacked his head mid-flight.

His teammates came and said some things,
But Billy could not hear.
His ears were covered all the way.
He longed to disappear.

His cheeks were warm, his chest felt tight,
His feet were dragging slow.
He could not bring his head up high.
His heart felt awfully low.

He walked into his house at last,
Back from this dreadful day.
His mom came in to say "hello"
And saw it right away.

She saw his hands, his chest, his feet.
She saw the mud and stress.
She pulled him close to her and said,
"I'm with you in this mess."

The whole bad day came out just then.
He told her every bit.
The fall, the quiz, the friends, the game.
"I just wanted to quit!"

"That does sound hard," sweet momma said.
Her heart was overflowing.
"Lets do what we do best of all,
Let's stay, instead of going."

They sat real still; they found some calm.
They practiced their deep breathing.
They did not run, or rush, or force.
They took some time for healing.

"You know what I think this stuff is?"
  She took some mud to show.
"I think I've seen this stuff before.
  I'll help you let it go."

"I've had this mud on me," she shared,
"It's really not so rare.
It's name is shame – it comes and goes
When we are unaware.

"Unaware of false thoughts and words,
 They sting us like a bee.
 It sometimes even makes me think
'There's something wrong with me.'"

"I thought those words today," he said.
"I thought that they were true!"
"Now, let me tell you," Momma said,
"There's *nothing* wrong with you."

"Is it so wrong to skip and trip?
Is it so wrong to fall?
Is it so wrong to fail a quiz?
It's *fine* to miss a ball."

"You'd still be you if trouble came
A-knockin' at your door.
It doesn't change your worth one bit
To fall down on the floor."

Bill breathed a big clean breath in deep
His cheeks – they felt alright.
He could not feel the shame mud now.
His heart felt whole and light.

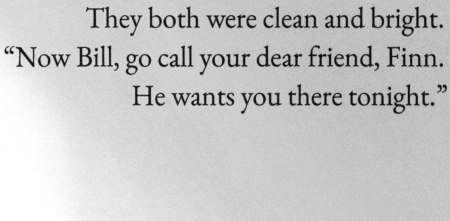

Mom took a big deep breath in, too.
They both were clean and bright.
"Now Bill, go call your dear friend, Finn.
He wants you there tonight."

She said that Finn had hardly stopped
His calls to his mom's phone.
"And your coach called to let you know.
That you are not alone."

"One drop after a long, hard game
Does not mean you're to blame.
The whole team wanted you to know
They like you just the same."

Bill smiled so wide it reached his eyes.
This day was not so sad.
"It *is* alright to make mistakes.
It doesn't mean I'm bad."

"I'll walk you to your best friend Finn's.
He missed you and your fun."
They breathed the freedom in the air.
And shame mud? There was none.

Discussion Questions
for
SHAME MUD

written by Jamie Jensen and illustrated by Dustin Baird

◆

1. Have you ever felt shame before? What was it like? Did it have an end?

2. Billy felt shame like it was thick mud. How do you feel shame in your body?

3. The story shows how shame is triggered for Billy as a boy, but do girls get triggered to shame in the same way? How is it different?

4. How did Billy get rid of the shame mud that was on him? Why was that so powerful? How can you get free from shame?

5. Do you have a trusted adult you can talk to about your shame mud with? Have they ever felt shame before?

CPSIA information can be obtained
at www.ICGtesting.com
Printed in the USA
BVHW060814051222
653468BV00009B/128